BASEBALL FROM A TO Z

By Michael P. Spradlin

Illustrated by Macky Pamintuan

HARPER

An Imprint of HarperCollinsPublishers

A

Ace. The best pitcher on each team is the ace of the pitching staff.

**Ballpark.** The ballpark is where baseball games are played. It's a fun place to spend the day!

Catcher. The catcher squats behind home plate and catches each ball thrown by the pitcher.

Dugout. The dugout is the bench area where the players sit while waiting for their turn at bat. There are two dugouts on the field, one for each team.

Error. If a fielder misses the ball, he can be charged with an error.

Foul Ball. A foul ball is hit into foul territory, outside the foul lines that are marked on the field.

WIN!

Grounder. A ball hit sharply on the ground is called a grounder.

Home Run. When the batter hits the ball over the outfield fence, the batter and all other runners on base get to score.

Infield. The infield is the part of the field inside the base paths. It is shaped like a diamond.

Jersey. *A special shirt is worn by each player to show what team he is on.*

Knuckleball. A knuckleball is a special pitch that darts and dips on its way toward home plate. The pitcher grips the ball with his knuckles, giving it a crazy spin when thrown.

Line Drive. A line drive is a ball hit hard on a straight Line.

Mascot. The home team has a mascot. It leads the cheers!

K K MVP GO TEAM! K K

	1	2	3	4	5	6
TORS	O	O	O	O	O	O
OME	O	I	I	O	O	O

AT BAT
21

LL

 **No-Hitter.** A no-hitter is a game in which the pitcher does not allow the opposing team to get any hits. No-hitters are very rare.

Outfielder. There are three outfielders who try to catch balls hit in the air over the infielders' heads. They are in left, center, and right field.

 **Pitcher.** The pitcher stands on the dirt mound in the middle of the infield and tries to get each batter out.

 **Quick Release.** It's good for a catcher to have a quick release, which means he can catch and throw the ball very fast. A catcher with a quick release keeps the other team's baserunners from stealing bases.

 **Rookie.** A rookie is a player who is in his first year of play. The best new player in each league every year wins the Rookie of the Year award.

**Shortstop.** The shortstop is the infielder who plays between second and third base. He can help throw runners out at any base—or even make a double play!

Tag. When a runner tries to run to the next base, the fielder must either "tag him out" before he reaches the base by touching him with the ball inside his glove or he must step on the base with the ball in his glove before the runner does.

Umpire. Umpires decide whether a runner is safe or out, whether a batted ball is fair or foul, and whether a pitch is a strike or a ball.

 **Visiting Team.** At each baseball game the home team plays against a team that has traveled from another ballpark.

Walk. When a pitch is outside the strike zone, it is called a ball by the umpire. When a pitcher throws four balls, the batter gets to go to first base safely.

Extra Innings. Extra innings are played when the score is tied at the end of nine innings.

Youth League. Baseball is a fun sport played by all ages. Most boys and girls first play baseball or softball in a youth league.

Strike Zone. To be in the strike zone, a pitch must be directly above home plate, no higher than the batter's shoulders or lower than his knees.

Now you know your

BASEBALL ALPHABET!

On your next trip to the ballpark, see if you can find other
baseball words from A to Z!

To Jeffrey T. Rogg, a Hall of Fame friend
—M.P.S.

For Uncle Allen, the best baseball fan I know.
—M.P.

Baseball from A to Z
Text copyright © 2010 by Michael P. Spradlin
Illustrations copyright © 2010 by Macky Pamintuan

Manufactured in China.

Library of Congress Cataloging-in-Publication Data
Spradlin, Michael P.
    Baseball from A to Z / by Michael Spradlin ; illustrated by Macky Pamintuan.
        p.   cm.
    ISBN 978-0-06-124081-2
    1. Baseball—Juvenile literature.   2. Alphabet books—Specimens.   I. Pamintuan, Macky, ill.   II. Title.
GV867.5.S67   2010   2009001399
796.357—dc22   CIP
                                                                                                         AC

Design by Stephanie Bart-Horvath
10   11   12   13   14   SCP   10   9   8   7   6   5   4   3   2   1
❖
First Edition